Too boring

Stephanie got twenty-five points on the "Cautious or Carefree?" quiz, which meant she was daring. Kate got seventeen points, and I got eighteen, which put us right in the middle. But poor Patti ended up with so few points that for her score the article said, "Are you still breathing? You'd better loosen up, fast!"

"Oh, dear," Patti mumbled. She blushed a bright red. "I don't know how you three can stand me — I don't know how anybody can stand me!" she wailed. "I'm too boring to live!"

Look for these and other books
in the Sleepover Friends Series:

Patti's New Look

Susan Saunders

AN
APPLE
PAPERBACK

SCHOLASTIC INC.
New York Toronto London Auckland Sydney

ISBN 0-590-40644-2

12 11 10 9 8 7 6 5 4   9/8 0 1 2 3/9

Printed in the U.S.A.   11

First Scholastic printing, February 1988

Chapter 1

"Is it ever going to stop?" Kate Beekman cupped her hands around her eyes and stared through the window at the snow swirling under the street lamp. The rest of us were lying on Stephanie Green's black-and-white rug, stuffing our faces, and reading teen magazines.

"Do you think Kevin's really in love with Marcy?" Patti Jenkins put down the magazine she was holding and looked concerned.

"If he is, he has a funny way of showing it!" Kate turned around and nodded knowingly. "He's been out with Tanya Colter at least three times recently — I saw it in *Confidentially Yours* at the supermarket."

"Tanya's great-looking — I especially like the

way she does her hair." Stephanie slicked her own curly black hair back on the sides and sucked in her cheeks.

"Kevin is too good for Tanya," Kate said firmly. She leaned down to scoop up Cinders, Stephanie's kitten.

Cinders is a brother to Kate's kitten, Fredericka. Stephanie, Patti, and I — I'm Lauren Hunter — had wanted to give Kate a calico kitten for her birthday. My mother found one for free in an ad in the newspaper. But she ended up with the calico's brothers and sister as well.

"I couldn't let them go to the pound," Mom had explained. "I figured we could find them good homes."

And we did — *our* homes. Cinders is coal black; my kitten, Rocky (to go with Bullwinkle, my family's dog), is black and white; and Patti's Adelaide is black and white, too. Patti's parents don't like pets, but they couldn't resist Adelaide.

"I think Marcy's too boring for Kevin," I broke in, grabbing the last peanut-butter-chocolate-chip cookie on the plate. "She reminds me of Karla Stamos."

The other girls burst out laughing because Karla Stamos is the dullest girl in our class. "Come on,

Lauren — Marcy Monroe and Karla? A movie star and a grind?"

"They both wear a lot of brown — nobody wears brown! They're both always talking about improving their minds and how they can't stand rock music — they only listen to classical. And they both squint," I pointed out. "I rest my case."

"I think Marcy wears contact lenses," Patti said.

"So what if she doesn't like rock?" said Kate. She put Cinders down on the bed, where he curled into a small, neat ball. "I still think Marcy's beautiful. And did you see the way she and Kevin kissed on *Made for Each Other* last Tuesday? That must mean something."

"Not at all," Stephanie told her. "They're actors! It's their business to fake stuff and make you believe it. Of course, if you'd ever done any acting yourself, you'd learn to spot a phony a mile off. . . ."

"I'm not sure a couple of lines in the class play counts as acting," Kate said.

"I also did some acting in the city. Enough to know what's real," Stephanie said huffily. Kate raised an eyebrow, but Stephanie ignored her. "And there's no way Kevin DeSpain's in love with Marcy Monroe in real life."

"You're probably right," Patti said sadly, picking up the magazine again and studying the photograph of Kevin as this month's "Teen Dream" in *Star Turns*. "He's awfully cute. And tall, too."

Patti's the tallest girl in fifth grade, so she's very aware of height.

"It says he likes to take romantic walks on the beach at Malibu, and surf, and sail to Catalina Island." Kate had put on her glasses to read over Patti's shoulder.

"Is there anything in this issue except California and Kevin?" Stephanie said impatiently.

Right now Stephanie likes blond guys more than dark-haired ones like Kevin. She has a crush on a conceited blond seventh-grader named Donald Foster, who lives in the house between Kate's and mine.

Patti turned the page — and blushed. "It's an article about kissing."

"What about kissing?" Stephanie reached for the magazine.

"Can we postpone it for a second? We're out of food!" I complained.

"Kissing is more important than food," Stephanie said.

"To you, maybe. Besides, I know more about kissing than the rest of you do." Not that I've had

4

actual experience, but I've got an older brother who has, and I've heard things. "I'll go for food!"

I picked up the empty plate and tiptoed down the dark hall to raid the Greens' kitchen. Stephanie's parents were already asleep.

I'm almost as used to Stephanie's house as I am to my own, or Kate's. Kate and I are practically next-door neighbors, since there's only Donald's house between us on Pine Street. We've been best friends since kindergarten, which is when the Friday-night sleepovers started. In the early days we dressed up in our moms' clothes and played "Grown-Ups," or "Let's Pretend." Kate's dad named us the Sleepover Twins, and it was just the two of us for ages.

Then, in fourth grade, Stephanie moved from the city to a new house at the end of Pine Street. She and I got to be friends because we were both in Mr. Civello's fourth-grade class. First I stopped by her house after school, then she began visiting me at my house.

Kate and Stephanie didn't get along so well at first. Kate thought Stephanie had a snobby attitude about being from the city, and Stephanie thought Kate was bossy. But they got used to each other when Stephanie started coming to our sleepovers and inviting us to stay overnight at her house.

Patti Jenkins is the newest of the Sleepover Friends. She has only been in Riverhurst a few months. Before that, she lived in the city, too.

Although Patti and Stephanie aren't anything alike, they were friends when they went to the same school in kindergarten and first grade. Patti is quiet and shy, and lots of things embarrass her.

As I walked back up the hall with more cookies and a bowl of caramel popcorn, I could hear her giggling nervously.

"I feel dumb kissing a pillow!" Kate was protesting as I came through the door.

She and Patti had their arms wrapped around pillows in black, white, and red cases, Stephanie's favorite color combination. Stephanie was reading from the kissing article in *Star Turns*.

"It says the main thing is to relax — relax your lips," Stephanie told them. She put down the magazine and picked up her own pillow. "Get yours off the bed, Lauren," she said to me.

"I think I'll just watch," I replied.

"Maybe if I close my eyes," Kate was muttering.

"Pretend you're kissing somebody you really like," Stephanie suggested.

Kate really likes Royce Mason, a tall, skinny seventh-grader.

6

Kate closed her eyes, and so did Patti. They both puckered their lips loosely. . . .

Kate opened her eyes and shook her head. "If the first boy I kiss is this soft and fat, he's the wrong one anyway." She gave her pillow a punch and threw it down on the floor. Patti put hers down, too, looking relieved.

"Roger used to practice on his arm," I reported. Roger's my older brother. He went through this stage a few years ago. "It must be a good way to learn, because he's always done okay with girls."

"I'll try it." Kate rolled up the sleeves of her sweat shirt, loosened her lips for a second, and kissed her forearm with a smack.

Stephanie rolled her eyes. "You don't have to make so much noise about it," she scolded.

"It's better than pillows," Kate said, "but I doubt seriously that it's anything like the real thing. Let's watch some TV — there's a festival of classics on channel twenty-one."

Kate is a real movie freak who'd like to direct her own films some day.

Stephanie blocked Kate from the television set. "We have to practice. You never can tell when we might need to know how to kiss — maybe sooner than you think."

7

"Like next Friday at Ekhart's Rink?" Kate snorted. "With Mr. and Mrs. Sykes sitting there? Give me a break, Stephanie!"

Mr. and Mrs. Sykes are Jane Sykes' parents. Jane is in 5B, Mrs. Mead's fifth-grade class, and so are the four of us. Winter vacation was starting the next Friday, and Jane had asked the girls in 5B — thirteen in all — to a huge sleepover at her house to celebrate.

Her parents were taking us to Ekhart's Ice-skating Rink that evening. And it was a pretty good bet that some of the boys we knew would go, too.

"Donald's not going to hang around with a bunch of lowly fifth-graders," Kate went on. "And you wouldn't be interested in kissing anybody else, would you, Stephanie? Could I please see that magazine?"

She pried it out of Stephanie's hands and turned the page. "Here's a quiz — 'Are You Cautious or Carefree?' Let's take it!"

"Let's!" Stephanie dug through her desk and came up with pencils and red notepaper for each of us.

"Okay, here goes," said Kate. "First question: 'You'll be spending Saturday with a new friend from school. When she asks you what you'd like to do, you reply: a. I think it would be fun to just play it by ear; b. I've made a list of things we could choose from; or c. Let's go to a movie.' "

"Definitely a." Stephanie scribbled on her piece of paper. "I always like playing it by ear."

I shook my head. "What if the new friend has rotten taste? *C*," I said positively.

"*B*," said Patti at the same time, then looked surprised that no one had agreed.

Kate wrote her answer down, too, and went on to the next question.

" 'While you're shopping with your friends, you try on an outfit that looks great on you, but is different from anything you've ever worn. Would you: a. ask your friends and other people in the store what they think before you make up your mind; b. buy the outfit and feel great every time you put it on; c. hang it back up, because you know you'd never have the nerve to wear it.' "

"Hmmm — probably *a*," I said, writing down my answer.

"*B*," said Stephanie. "I'm the one who's wearing it, so who needs to ask anybody else anything?"

"*C*?" murmured Patti uncertainly.

"Question number three," said Kate. " 'When you go to dinner at a new restaurant and discover there's nothing on the menu that you recognize, do

9

you: a. look on it as an adventure and pick something yourself; b. ask the waiter to bring the closest thing he's got to a hamburger; c. decide you're not hungry and couldn't possibly eat a thing.' "

"A," I said right away. I'm pretty interested in most food.

Stephanie made a face. "B. It's clear that you've never seen baked snails, Lauren."

Patti listened to both of us, then wrote her answer down without saying a word. So did Kate.

"Ready?" Kate read the next question. " 'A friend calls on Thursday to invite you on an exciting trip that weekend with her and her parents. You: a. start cramming stuff into a suitcase — you can hardly wait! b. tell her you can't — you'd need a lot more time to get ready; c. think about it for a while, then call her back and say yes.' "

"Sounds great — a!" Stephanie scrawled her answer.

"Probably c," I admitted. Sometimes it takes me a while to make up my mind.

Patti frowned. She was beginning to look worried.

There were ten questions in all, each with three possible answers. When we'd finished, Kate told us how many points each answer was worth. Then we totaled them up.

Stephanie got twenty-five points, which meant she was daring and carefree, although the article warned that maybe she could stand to give her decisions a little more thought. Kate got seventeen points, and I got eighteen, which put us right in the middle: "It's smart to be sensible, but don't overdo it." But poor Patti ended up with so few points that for her score the article said, "Are you still breathing? You'd better loosen up, fast!"

Stephanie reached over to put her fingers on Patti's wrist. "There's still a pulse . . ." she teased.

"Oh, dear," Patti mumbled. She blushed a bright red. "I don't know how you three can stand me — I don't know how anybody can stand me!" she wailed. "I'm too boring to live!"

"Patti, it's a dumb test!" Kate said quickly, pitching the magazine across the room.

"Sure it is." Stephanie picked up the magazine and stuffed it into the wastepaper basket. Then she switched on the TV set. Two old movie stars were kissing in black and white. "Hey — grab your pillows, girls! We can kiss along with Clark Gable!"

"Take me in your arms, my darling," Kate murmured in a husky voice. She picked up Cinders and smooched his nose. Cinders returned the favor by licking Kate's glasses.

Kate and Stephanie and I giggled. But Patti still looked stricken. Once she gets something in her mind — like the time she decided she was bad luck — she won't let it drop.

Chapter 2

That Saturday morning, we went shopping. Mrs. Green pulled her car over to the curb in front of Dandelion on Main Street. "My hair appointment is at ten," she said, "so I'll pick you up here around eleven-fifteen."

"We'll probably go for sodas when we're through here, Mom," Stephanie told her. "We'll meet you in front of Charlie's."

"All right — have a good time." Mrs. Green waved good-bye as we climbed out of the car.

We struggled through the snowdrifts to the steps of the store. Dandelion sells really great kids' clothes, and the big window in front was full of bright-colored swimsuits.

"Who can even think about bathing suits at this time of year?" Kate grumbled.

"Just looking at them makes me colder," I agreed.

"Be glad they're there," Stephanie said, pushing open the front door. "That means all the winter stuff's on sale!"

"Good morning, girls. What are you shopping for today?" Mrs. Martin, the owner of Dandelion seems to know exactly what kids in Riverhurst will be doing next. She always has lots of good recommendations.

"Something to wear to a skating party next Friday," Kate answered.

"Pile your coats on the chair and take a look at the sweaters and tights against the back wall," Mrs. Martin suggested. "Forty percent off all the items with red tags."

Stephanie dug through the stacks of sweaters until she came up with one that had red and white squiggles on it. "Perfect with my black stretch pants," she said. "I'm going to try it on."

Kate picked out a sweater with yellow and green zigzags, and some dark-green leg warmers. I came up with a turquoise and black top, and Patti took a long, hooded navy-blue sweater dotted with white snowflakes.

14

We were heading for the dressing rooms when Patti murmured in disgust, "Navy blue! Why do I always end up with navy blue? If you think Karla Stamos is dull, try me! Go ahead," she said to Kate and me. "I'll be there in a second."

"Why did we ever take that stupid test!" I whispered to Kate.

Patti had an armful of clothes when she finally came into the dressing room: an electric-blue stretch jumpsuit, bright orange tights, a black western shirt with rhinestones all over the back, a belt made from a bike chain, and shiny yellow suspenders. She tried them all on, frowning at herself in the mirror.

We'd already decided on our own stuff, so we sat on the little wrought-iron chairs and watched. Patti ended up in a pink polka-dotted sweater, a poison-green miniskirt, and striped pink leggings. "What do you think?" she asked us.

Patti is slender, and she looks good in most clothes, but I wasn't sure about *these* clothes. "Well . . . uh — it's a great outfit," I replied.

"The colors are nice on you," Kate added.

"I think you look fantastic!" Stephanie said enthusiastically. "But isn't it expensive?"

"I have the money my grandmother gave me for Christmas," Patti said.

"Don't buy it if you're not going to wear it — you can't return sale stuff," Kate said. Kate is always practical.

"I'll wear it. And I'll feel great every time I do." Patti sounded exacty like the quiz! "What about the chain belt?"

"It's fine without it," I said hurriedly.

We paid for our clothes and slogged through the snow to Charlie's Soda Fountain at the other end of the block. At Charlie's, we always sit in the last booth, and we always order the same things: Kate gets a float with two scoops of vanilla ice cream, Stephanie orders a chocolate milk shake, I get a banana smoothie, and Patti has a lime freeze.

So when the waitress brought the menus, Kate said, "Thanks, but we don't need them. We already know what we want."

"I'd like to see a menu," Patti said.

We waited as she read it through. "The Secret Weapon, please," Patti told the waitress at last.

The Secret Weapon is one of Charlie's special inventions. It's supposed to be a mixture of everything in the place. And you have to have a cast-iron stomach to even try it. *I'm* the one with the cast-iron stomach, not Patti.

"The Secret Weapon, huh?" the waitress repeated, looking Patti over doubtfully. "You sure?" When Patti nodded, the waitress said, "Oka-a-ay. . . ." She scribbled on her green pad and added, "You know, if you finish it, you get a second one free — compliments of Charlie's."

"Has anybody ever finished two?" Kate asked.

"A year or so ago, one of the high-school boys drank one and a half," the waitress answered. "What was his name? Bug, or Lug, or something. . . ."

"Tug Keeler?" He weighs about two hundred and fifty pounds, and he's a tackle on the Riverhurst High football team!

"Tug Keeler — that's right. Didn't see him for quite a while after that." She took the menu and walked over to the counter.

If the Secret Weapon had wiped out Tug Keeler, what would it do to Patti? We gazed at the stained glass in the window next to us, thinking our own thoughts, until the waitress came back with our orders. "Float, shake, and smoothie." She sat them down in front of Kate, Stephanie, and me. "And — ta da — the Secret Weapon!" She plunked a glass down in front of Patti.

All four of us stared at the Secret Weapon. The glass was tall and frosted, with exploding fireworks stamped on it in red. The drink was thick and dark, kind of a brownish-purple color. Even though there were ice cubes floating in it, it seemed to be bubbling, like some sort of magic potion!

"Do you think the purple is grape juice? Or cherry juice?" Kate wondered out loud.

"Maybe it's prune juice! Yuck!" Stephanie murmured. "Are you really going to drink that?" she asked Patti.

"I want to try new things," Patti said determinedly.

"But wouldn't a strawberry freeze have been new enough?" Kate wanted to know.

Patti shook her head. "Anybody want a sip before I start?"

Stephanie and Kate hurriedly sipped their own drinks.

"Lauren?"

"Not before lunch," I said hastily.

"Well . . . here goes." Patti took a deep breath, picked up the glass — and drank the Secret Weapon straight down! Then she swallowed a couple of times, hard.

"Wow! What did it taste like?" Stephanie asked her.

"Sweet," Patti said. "It was very sweet." She shuddered a little. "It wasn't so bad," she added, swallowing again. "Thick — kind of coats your throat, like cough medicine."

The waitress stopped at our table a few minutes later. "Can I bring you anything else, kids?" Then she noticed Patti's empty glass. "I never would have believed it!" she exclaimed. "Ready for your second?"

"Why not?" Patti said bravely.

"Patti, you've already had the new experience. I wouldn't push my luck if I were you," Kate warned.

"I won't drink the whole thing," Patti said.

Patti took only a couple of sips of the second Secret Weapon before pushing the glass away. She wasn't saying much — she seemed very thoughtful. Patti rested her hand on her stomach for a minute or so, as though she were trying to calm it down.

Kate checked her watch. "It's almost eleven-fifteen. Your mom'll be here soon, Stephanie."

"Let's pay and go outside," Stephanie said.

We were walking down the front steps of Charlie's with our Dandelion shopping bags when someone yelled, "Hey — girls!"

"Mark Freedman — across the street!" Stephanie declared.

"And Larry Jackson, and Henry Larkin!" They're all boys in our class. They'd been in Mimi's Pizza —

19

I could see tomato sauce on Henry's white parka from where we were standing.

"Get 'em!" Larry shouted. The boys started scooping up handfuls of snow and packing it into snowballs.

"Take cover!" Kate ordered.

We dashed up the sidewalk, giggling. We crouched down behind a parked car and started making snowballs ourselves.

"YEOW!" The boys attacked, throwing snowballs as they ran across the street and rushed the parked car.

We forced them back. You wouldn't think so to look at her, but Stephanie has a great pitching arm. She got Larry on the ear and Henry Larkin in the back of the head as he retreated up the sidewalk.

"Regroup, men!" Mark bellowed. "Regr —"

Poom! I got Mark right in the face!

Stephanie stood up. "They're on the run!"

Kate grabbed as many snowballs as she could carry and followed Stephanie up the sidewalk after the boys.

"Come on, Patti!" I said, scrambling to my feet.

"I think I'll stay here with the packages," Patti said weakly, sinking slowly into a snowdrift.

"Are you okay?" I asked her.

20

"I . . . uh . . . actually . . . I don't feel too well," Patti admitted at last.

I took a closer look at her. She was slumped in the snow, and her face was pale and sort of splotchy.

"Yikes!" Stephanie shrieked. She and Kate were thundering back down the sidewalk in a hail of snowballs, the boys not far behind them.

"Don't just sit there — throw something!" Kate yelled at Patti and me.

I shook my head. "Patti's sick."

"What's the matter?" Kate kneeled in the snow to feel Patti's forehead — Kate's father is a doctor. "No fever, but she doesn't look great," Kate said to me in a lower voice. "Patti, stick out your tongue."

Next she'd be listening to Patti's heart! "Kate, it's the Secret Weapon," I said.

The boys charged, whooping and shouting and pelting us all with snowballs.

"Cut that out!" Stephanie screeched. "Patti's not feeling well!"

"Listen, if we hit you too hard with a snowball, or something . . ." Mark started to apologize to Patti.

"It's not that — it's her stomach," I explained. "Patti drank one whole Secret Weapon and part of a second."

"You're kidding!" The boys stared expectantly

at Patti. It looked as if they were waiting for her to explode.

"Kyle Hubbard drank part of one once on a dare," Larry told us.

"He thought he was going to throw up for hours afterward. Is that how you feel, Patti?" Henry Larkin wanted to know.

"Please," Patti murmured queasily. "I'm trying not to think about it."

"Yeah, thanks for sharing that with us, Henry," Stephanie muttered.

"Stand back — give Patti some air," Kate said to the boys.

"Stephanie, where could your mother be?" I asked anxiously.

Mark climbed to the top of a big pile of snow to look up and down the street. "Here comes a red car," he reported at last. "Yep — it's your mom, Stephanie."

When the car had rolled to a stop beside us, Mark pulled open the back door. While Stephanie told her mom what was going on, Kate and I shoved our packages onto the shelf behind the back seat and helped Patti in. She sat there kind of hunched over, swallowing a lot.

"Oh, dear," Mrs. Green said after one quick

glance. "We'll have you home in no time, Patti."

A last snowball burst against the window on my side as we drove away — Larry couldn't resist a moving target. But things were very quiet on the way to Patti's house. I think we were all waiting to see if she was going to be sick.

Once we'd gotten Patti — and her package — safely indoors, Mrs. Green asked us, "Why in the world did she finish the drink if it was so awful?"

"It's a long story, Mrs. Green," Kate said. "It all started with a magazine quiz."

"And trying new things," I added.

"It just doesn't sound like Patti," Mrs. Green said, shaking her head.

"That's the whole point, Mom," said Stephanie.

"I'll bet she never wears that outfit," Kate predicted.

Chapter
3

On Saturday evening, Stephanie spoke to Patti on the phone — Patti said she was feeling a lot better. By Monday, Patti seemed to have forgotten about the quiz and was back to normal: she was wearing her old navy-blue and white striped sweater, and she drank her usual container of milk with lunch in the school cafeteria, instead of something weird, like pineapple juice.

Stephanie, Kate, Patti, and I had almost finished eating when Mark Freedman and some other boys walked by. "That's her," Mark said suddenly. "Patti Jenkins — she's the one who drank *two* Secret Weapons!"

The group swung around and stopped at our table. It was Mark, and Larry, of course, since they're

24

always together, and Bobby Krieger from 5C, whom Kate used to like, and Alan Reese and Todd Farrell from 5A.

"Wow!" Bobby said. "Two of 'em?"

"Only one, and a couple of sips," Patti mumbled, blushing a bright red because she was the center of attention.

"Still," Bobby insisted. "A girl who can finish a whole Secret Weapon!"

"I guess you're all going to sleep over at Jane Sykes's on Friday?" Alan asked us.

"Sure," said Stephanie.

"Bobby and I might be at Ekhart's Rink that night," he said. "And Todd — he's Jane's cousin, you know."

Todd nodded shyly.

"Did somebody say something about Ekhart's on Friday? Scoot over, Lauren." It was Pete Stone, squeezing into an empty chair at our table. Pete's in our room. He has curly, dark-brown hair and light green eyes. We're sort of interested in each other, since we got stuck in an elevator together on a field trip to the museum. "Sounds good to me." He gave us all a big grin.

"Yeah, I'll probably be there," Mark said.

"Me, too," said Larry.

Henry Larkin trotted by then. "Come on, guys —

let's go to the gym and shoot a few baskets."

The whole group trotted after him, and Pete jumped up, too. "See you!"

As soon as the boys were out of earshot, Kate nudged me with her elbow. "If looks could kill," she murmured.

We all knew who Kate meant: Jenny Carlin, who's also in 5B. Jenny had a crush on Pete, and she hated it that Pete liked me. The thing is, I don't think Pete ever liked her, because Jenny is just too pushy. Anyway, I guess she had seen Pete talking to us, because she was glaring in our direction. She was sitting with Angela Kemp, a Jenny Carlin-in-training, who glared at us, too.

"Jenny Carlin's somebody who could use a little practice on her act," Stephanie said. She imitated Jenny's high squeaky voice: "Oh, Pe-e-ete — you're the funniest guy!"

"Ick," said Kate, staring straight at Jenny until she stopped looking at us.

"Is Todd nice?" Patti asked then.

"Very. I hadn't really noticed before, but he's cuter than he was last year," Stephanie said. Todd had been in Mr. Civello's fourth-grade class with Stephanie and me. "He's so shy around girls that I hardly ever get a good look at him."

26

"He's a lot taller than he was, too," I added. Todd was quite a bit taller than Patti now — he was tallest in the group of boys he was with, and Pete's no shorty. Thinking about it, I decided Todd and Patti had a few things in common, like height, and shyness, and blushing. "I'd forgotten that he's Jane's cousin," I said.

"I wonder who else will show up at the rink?" asked Kate. She and Stephanie and I started talking about the skating party and the sleepover. Patti watched Todd until he'd disappeared through the doors at the end of the cafeteria. Maybe she was starting to look forward to the party, instead of worrying about whether she'd be boring.

Whatever she had been thinking about then, Patti was really upset when she got the news that she wouldn't even be able to go to the party. She told us before school the next morning. "I can't go to Jane's — I found out last night that I'll be having company."

"Who?" Stephanie asked. It was snowing again, so practically everybody was crammed into the school auditorium, waiting for the bell to ring for class.

"This girl named Karen Lawson," Patti answered glumly. "Her parents and my parents used to teach at the same university years ago. And we spent a few summers together when we were little kids. Then the Lawsons moved to California."

"So what's Karen doing here now?" I asked.

"Her sister Lisa's a junior in high school. Lisa and Mr. and Mrs. Lawson are going to be visiting colleges she might apply to next year," Patti explained.

"So they're dumping Karen on you," Stephanie said.

"I guess so," said Patti.

"What's Karen like?" Kate asked.

"The last time I saw her she was short, thin, really quiet — she was always reading," Patti answered.

"Sounds like fun," Stephanie said, rolling her eyes. "Just how long is she staying?"

"The whole ten days of vacation."

Stephanie groaned.

"Well, it's not fair that you can't go to the sleep-over!" Kate exclaimed indignantly. "I'm going to talk to Jane about inviting Karen, too!"

"Oh, no, please don't, Kate!" Patti wailed. "How embarrassing!"

But Kate is very strong-minded. She was already cutting across the auditorium to where Jane was standing with some other girls. Kate talked, Jane

28

glanced over at us, and back at Kate. Kate shook her head, Jane nodded.

Then the bell rang. All the kids started hurrying out of the auditorium toward their classrooms. Stephanie, Patti, and I ran to catch up with Kate.

"What did Jane say?" Stephanie asked her.

"No problem — Karen can come," Kate replied. "There's plenty of room, since we're all going to be sleeping on the floor anyway. And after I described Karen to Jane, we both decided it wouldn't make much difference whether she was there or not — probably nobody will even notice her."

"That's great!" Stephanie and I squealed.

"Thanks, Kate." Patti was beaming.

The Lawsons' plane from California was landing at the airport at three on Friday afternoon. Patti and her parents and her little brother, Horace, were driving into the city to meet the Lawsons. Then Karen was coming back to Riverhurst with the Jenkinses, while her sister and parents were catching a smaller plane to a college town upstate.

It only takes an hour and a half to drive from Riverhurst to the city, or the other way around. Jane's party wasn't starting until five-thirty, which left plenty of time for Patti and Karen to get there.

I was a little late when Mom dropped me off at the bottom of the Sykeses' driveway. They live in a big split-level that rambles all over the side of a hill. I'd only been to the house a few times before, to some of Jane's birthday parties. I climbed the stone front steps and rang the doorbell.

Jane opened the door. "Hi, Lauren!"

"Hi, Jane — am I late?"

"No more than usual," Kate answered. She and Stephanie had been hanging around the front hall.

"Patti here?" I asked them.

"Not yet," Stephanie answered.

"We're sleeping in the living room." Jane led me down the hall to a huge, square room with windows all along one side. The furniture was pushed back against the walls, so there'd be space for everyone's sleeping bag. Karen Lawson would make fourteen people in all.

"Drop your stuff and come on to the kitchen," Jane told me. "We're going to eat first and leave for the rink around six-thirty."

"Patti should be here by then," I said to Kate and Stephanie.

"It's probably just traffic," said Kate. "We're in the corner by the TV set."

I recognized Stephanie's canvas tote and Kate's backpack, so I put my own sleeping bag, backpack, and skates down next to them.

"Jenny Carlin's all the way on the other side of the couch, next to Angela," Stephanie added in an undertone. "You sleep next to the wall, so Kate and I can protect you if Jenny turns into a vampire in the middle of the night."

"Stop it!" All of us were giggling.

"Wait until you see what Jenny's got on," Stephanie told me.

"Who else is here?" I asked.

"Sally Mason, Robin Becker, Erin Wilson, Nancy Hersh, Karla . . . practically everybody. Come on — the kitchen's this way."

Kate and I followed Stephanie through the living room and across the dining room to the kitchen.

Chapter 4

When my brother Roger first heard about Jane's sleepover, he groaned, "Poor Dennis Sykes! It's bad enough having four of you squirts overnight, but thirteen? Forget it!"

But Jane's older brother Dennis didn't seem to be having such a terrible time. He was passing platters of sandwiches around, while Mrs. Sykes dumped big bags of barbecue potato chips and Cheese Doodles into wire baskets, and Mr. Sykes poured Dr. Pepper and Cherry Coke into glasses.

"Hi, Lauren!" Erin and Nancy and Sally Mason called.

"Yes . . . hello, Lauren. Glad you could come." Mrs. Sykes was looking a little frazzled. She checked out the long table, murmuring, "Chips, dips, vegetable sticks, potato salad. Girls, please take a plate and help yourselves to everything," she added to Kate, and Stephanie, and me. "The drinks are on the counter, and there are loads of brownies in the refrigerator when you're finished. Lester, let's sit down in the den for a minute." She reached for Mr. Sykes's arm and led him away. "We'll need all our strength later."

I turned toward the table, and there was Jenny Carlin, practically drooling on Dennis's arm when he offered her a sandwich. I saw what Stephanie meant about vampires — Jenny was dressed all in black! She was wearing a black sweat shirt with glitter on the sleeves and black pants.

Angela Kemp had on a blue outfit. She nodded at me, but Jenny was too busy watching Dennis to even frown.

"Somebody probably told her black is grown-up," Kate whispered in my ear.

"Not when your skin is green," I whispered back. Jenny makes me act hateful.

"I'm going to my room to watch the hockey game, Mom," Dennis said, plunking the sandwich platter down in the middle of the table.

"All right, but don't get too involved," Mrs. Sykes warned over her shoulder. "We're leaving for the skating rink in about an hour, and we'll need you then."

Jane handed Stephanie, Kate, and me forks and napkins and Dr. Peppers, and we slid onto one of the long benches on either side of the table.

Jenny was flashing Dennis a winning smile as he left the kitchen.

"Get real!" Kate muttered. "I mean, she's barely eleven, and he's sixteen!"

"Jenny is really operating tonight," Stephanie said in a low voice. "Better keep your eye on Pete."

It took a while for everybody to finish eating. Then it was almost time to leave. We took turns piling into the nearest bathroom to comb our hair.

Then Mr. and Mrs. Sykes organized us into two groups. The larger group was riding to the rink with Dennis and Mr. Sykes in Mr. Sykes's van. The smaller group would go with Jane and Mrs. Sykes in her car.

"I want to ride in the van," Stephanie said to Kate and me, "to watch Jenny in action."

"I think she put on some eyeliner in the bathroom," I reported.

"You're kidding!" Kate peered hard at Jenny. "You're right!" she hissed. "There's a wiggly line on her right eyelid!"

But the three of us ended up in the car with Jane and her mom.

"I wonder what's happened to Patti?" Stephanie said as we climbed into the backseat with our skates. "She hates to be late."

"Patti Jenkins?" Mrs. Sykes said. "Her mother called a little while ago. The traffic coming from the airport was so heavy that they just got in. They'll grab a bite to eat and bring the girls to the skating rink."

"People can change a lot in two or three years," Stephanie said to us. "I wonder what Karen Lawson will be like."

"We'll find out soon," Kate replied.

Ekhart's was great that night. It wasn't too crowded, the ice was in good shape, and they were playing rock music instead of the usual corny polkas. And a bunch of the boys were already there. Mark and Larry and Henry were skating when we got inside, and Pete Stone walked into the rink while we were putting our skates on.

Pete's a really good skater, and I'm not bad, either — Roger taught me to skate when I was four. Pete and I tried skating our names on the ice for a while: *Pete Stone* is a lot easier to write than *Lauren Hunter*. Then Kate, Stephanie, Jane, Nancy, Sally, and I played crack-the-whip. Jenny Carlin was hanging on to the barrier around the ice, shrieking and pretending she was going to fall. Angela was hovering nearby.

"Jenny has one eye on Pete Stone and the other on Dennis Sykes," Stephanie pointed out. "No wonder she's having trouble. Her poor feet don't have a clue about which way she's going!"

Bobby Krieger and Alan Reese and Larry were speeding around the edge of the ice, Robin Becker and Mark were trying out fancy dance steps to the music, Todd Farrell was practicing jumps by himself, when Henry Larkin suddenly yelled, "Wow!"

He was staring at the entrance to the rink, so naturally everybody stopped what they were doing and turned around to look, too.

"Patti's here!" Jane Sykes said.

Patti was wearing her new outfit, just as she told us she would — the pink polka-dotted sweater, the green miniskirt, and striped pink leggings. And she looked terrific!

But Patti might as well have worn her old navy-blue sweater and jeans. And the rest of us could have dropped straight through the ice, for all the difference it would have made to the boys.

36

"Wow!" Henry said again, in case we'd missed it the first time.

"Wow!" Bobby Krieger echoed. "Who is *that*?"

Kate, Stephanie, and I looked at each other. "Karen Lawson?" Stephanie mouthed and clapped her hand to her forehead.

"Short, thin, really quiet — always reading," Patti had said about Karen Lawson.

"Well, she's still short," Kate murmured.

"But I wouldn't exactly call her thin, would you?" I said. In fact, Karen Lawson had a real *shape*.

"Is that a rubber mini?" Stephanie squeaked. "We read about rubber minis in *Style* — it said they're the latest fashion statement from southern California, remember? I've never seen one in person."

"It doesn't seem all that comfortable — she keeps tugging on the bottom of it," Kate pointed out.

Comfortable or not, the mini looked great. It was a deep red. Karen Lawson had on white leg warmers, and her sweater was red sprinkled with black lines and white circles and crosses, like a tic-tac-toe game. One of her arms was loaded with sparkling bangle bracelets that clinked as she moved, and a gold feather earring dangled from one ear . . . and she didn't even look tacky! Her hair was honey-colored, shoulder-length, and a mass of tight little waves. She had straight, dark eyebrows, bright blue eyes, and kind of pouty lips. And if that weren't enough, she had a *tan*, in the middle of winter!

Patti waved at us. "Stephanie, Lauren, Kate — come meet Karen!"

We had to push the boys out of the way: they were frozen with admiration. Even Pete had a really goofy grin on his face that made me want to kick him!

"So far, the only good thing about this is Jenny Carlin," Kate said.

Jenny was so freaked out by Karen Lawson that she'd forgotten to pretend she couldn't skate — she was gliding across the ice without a wobble.

"Karen," Patti said proudly, "these are my best friends. Kate, Stephanie, Lauren, this is Karen Lawson."

"I've heard so much about you from Patti," Karen said in a breathless little voice. "Aren't we going to have *fun*?"

Before any of us could say anything, she turned to her crowd of male admirers. "Is there anyone here who wouldn't mind spending a few minutes teaching me to skate?" she said helplessly, flicking a dark-blonde curl out of her face. "I don't even know how to put these things on properly," she pouted, swinging her rented skates back and forth by their laces.

Kate and Stephanie and I had to jump out of the way, or we would have been crushed to death in the stampede of boys.

Mark Freedman took Karen over to the bleachers, while Bobby Krieger explained in detail how to lace up her ice skates. Pete Stone even helped her put them on. And all of them stared at Karen the whole time, as if they were afraid she'd disappear.

"Gag me!" Stephanie said, making rude noises.

"Jenny Carlin had better take a lesson from Karen Lawson," Kate said.

"We'd all better," I said grimly.

Chapter
5

"Isn't Karen great?" Patti exclaimed to Kate, Stephanie, and me.

We were on our way back to the Sykeses' house from the skating rink. This time we were in the van; Karen was sitting in the front seat between Dennis and Mr. Sykes, talking Dennis's ear off about California while he drove. The other four of us were crammed into the small seat at the rear of the van.

"Yeah, great," I said glumly.

Jenny Carlin was in the seat in front of us, along with Angela, Karla, and Robin. She turned around and looked right at me. "Pete Stone certainly seemed to think so," she sniped. "He waved good-bye to her for so long, I was afraid his hand was going to fall off."

"Listen, Jenny . . .," Kate began, with a nasty gleam in her eye.

But Stephanie jabbed Kate with her elbow. "Karen's amazing!" Stephanie said enthusiastically. "She really livens things up!" I heard her hiss in Kate's ear, "Don't give Carlin the satisfaction."

Besides, Karen *was* amazing. Who could argue with that? She had managed to have all the boys eating out of her hand — or almost all of them: Todd Farrell wouldn't go near her — without making all the girls hate her. *I* didn't even hate her, and Pete had acted the goofiest. She couldn't help it if she was terrific-looking.

"Your new outfit is super," I said to Patti to change the subject.

"I wasn't going to wear it," Patti admitted, "but Karen said I absolutely had to. You know that quiz in the magazine? If Karen took it, I'm sure she'd score a perfect thirty! Being around her is really going to be good for me!"

Was it? I wondered. And what about the rest of us?

Back at the house, Mrs. Sykes had dished out the snacks. There was the usual caramel popcorn we always have at our own sleepovers, but there was fancier stuff, too, like tiny pepperoni pizzas Mrs.

Sykes had made herself, and shrimp dip, and a big cheddar cheese ball with olives and pimientos in it.

"Wonderful food, Jane," Karen said as she gracefully bit into a piece of pizza. "I love the cheese ball — there was one just like it at a party I went to in Malibu."

"You've been to Malibu?" Patti squeaked.

"I go all the time," Karen replied. "A couple of my friends live there."

"That's where all the movie stars have houses!" Nancy Hersh practically shrieked.

"Have you ever seen any stars?" Sally Mason asked.

Karen nodded, spreading more of the cheese ball on a cracker. "Um . . . Joel Kelly and Carter Grant — I've seen them jogging on the beach a couple of times."

"Wow!" said Angela Kemp. "They're my all-time favorite actors. I watch *Surftown* every week!"

Jenny Carlin scowled at Angela, but Angela was too excited to pay any attention to her leader. "What do they look like in person?" Angela wanted to know.

"Carter's really intense!" said Karen. "He's taller than he looks on TV, with a dark tan, and kind of sun-bleached hair."

Angela was hanging on Karen's every word, and Jenny looked mad enough to spit!

"But I think I like Joel better," Karen went on. "He's really easygoing and friendly — he'll stop and talk to anybody."

"Did he talk to you?" Even Karla Stamos sounded interested, and she usually pretends she never gets near a television set.

"Sure. Just to say hello, of course," Karen added quickly, as though she didn't want to be bragging.

"It'd be neat to live in California!" Erin Wilson said with a sigh.

"It is," Karen agreed. "The weather is fantastic — it usually never gets colder than fifty degrees, so you can swim for most of the year, or go windsurfing. . . ."

"Do you windsurf?" Dennis had come into the kitchen to grab a Coke, and he'd caught the tail end of the conversation. He windsurfs every summer at the lake.

"I'm just learning — it's totally awesome!" Karen told him. "I'm not very good yet, but I've got a Vinta sailboard, and a Gul wet suit, and a second-hand rig. . . ."

As Dennis launched into a discussion of windsurfing, and harnesses, and planing, and who knows what else, Karen looked fascinated, and Jenny was steaming.

But it was Kate who interrupted them. "What about Kevin DeSpain? Have you ever seen him hanging around Malibu?" She was leaning forward with that why-should-I-believe-a-word-you're-saying expression on her face.

"Uh — Kevin? I saw him with Marcy Monroe just last week, in a café on the beach," Karen answered. "Popcorn?" She passed the bowl to Kate.

"Kevin DeSpain! I would just die!" Robin Becker sighed. "Are you lucky!"

"I *knew* they really liked each other!" Patti said to Stephanie, her eyes sparkling.

"I'm tired!" Jenny Carlin announced loudly. She marched across the kitchen toward the living room.

"Yeah, I'd better hit the sack, too," Dennis said. "Good night."

" 'Night, Dennis."

Everybody grabbed some food and trooped into the living room. Jenny was rolling out her sleeping bag at one end of the couch. I spread mine out next to the wall. Kate was beside me, with Stephanie next, then Patti, and last Karen.

No sooner had *we* gotten arranged than there

was a lot of rearranging, with Angela Kemp moving her stuff from the couch to our side of the room. Karla and Nancy Hersh moved over, too. By the time everyone had switched around, Jenny was all by herself, which didn't make her any happier.

Then we changed into our sleep things. Karen had these funny blue pajamas, with long sleeves and a high neck decorated with lace.

"I would have expected something a little glitzier," Kate murmured to me.

Maybe Karen heard Kate, because she giggled suddenly. "Aren't these pj's too much? My mother bought them for me before the trip out. It's too cold here for me to sleep the way I usually do . . . in the raw . . ."

There were gasps from Angela and Karla, both of them draped in long nightshirts. Karla's was brown and beige stripes.

"What are the boys like in California?" Robin wanted to know.

"Great!" Karen said. "I'm seeing a really sharp guy named Randy Martin. He's older, thirteen."

"Thirteen!" Sally Mason was shocked.

"Yeah, he's a Libra, and I'm a Gemini, so we're perfect for each other."

"Do you believe in astrology?" Erin asked her.

"Why not? People have believed in it for thousands of years, and it sure works for me. Geminis are outgoing. They love to be doing new things, meeting new people — they like to get involved in lots of things at once. . . ." Karen cocked her head to one side and shrugged. "Is that me, or isn't it?"

"I was born on September eleventh," Karla said. "What sign is that?"

"You're a Virgo," Karen replied. "Virgos are hard workers. They're intelligent and serious. They always want to learn more."

"That's right!" Karla exclaimed.

"What she's saying is, Virgos are grinds," murmured Stephanie.

"You like good food . . ." Karen continued.

Jenny Carlin snickered. "You don't need astrology to know that." Karla's a little plump.

Karen ignored Jenny and went on, ". . . and good clothes."

Kate rolled her eyes. *All brown*, she mouthed.

"This month, you shouldn't worry if you're not able to satisfy your family, no matter how hard you try. Experiment with new ideas, go to new places," Karen advised Karla.

"I will," Karla said solemnly.

"What about me?" Jane Sykes asked. "My birth-day's July twenty-fourth."

"That's Leo," said Karen. "You're creative, good at art . . ."

"I paint," Jane said, nodding.

". . . you're generous, warm, understanding." Jane smiled, pleased.

"November third?" one of the other girls asked.

"What about March sixteenth?" I couldn't help myself, although I knew what Kate was thinking: There goes Lauren, letting her imagination run away with her again!

"March sixteenth — you're a Pisces, Lauren. You're always tuned in to the people around you."

Wasn't I always figuring out what my friends were thinking before they'd said a word?

"Pisces are dreamers," Karen went on, "and you have a strong imagination."

There was a snort from Kate.

"Well, it's true, isn't it?" I said under my breath.

"For you and all the millions of other people born on March sixteenth?" Kate hissed.

"A trip you've been counting on might not work out this month" — maybe the trip to my grand-mother's? — "but you'll make a new friend and smooth some ruffled feelings." I heard Kate give a thoughtful little "hmmmm," behind me.

"Where did you learn all this stuff?" Angela Kemp asked Karen.

"Oh, I've picked it up here and there. I know a really amazing astrologer named Zoltan, who studied in India. He has a bald head, covered with tattoos of the heavens," Karen answered.

"Neat!" said Angela.

"Doesn't anybody want to play Truth or Dare?" Jenny Carlin interrupted in a bored voice. I'm sure she had some horrible dare in mind for Karen.

"Truth or Dare! I haven't played that in so long, I'd forgotten about it completely!" Karen giggled.

"Would you rather play something else?" Jane asked apologetically.

"Just what do you do at parties in California?" Kate's left eyebrow was raised so high, it almost disappeared into her hair.

"Well, if it's a party with boys — we usually play seven minutes in heaven," Karen replied casually.

"Seven minutes in heaven? What's that?" Angela Kemp practically screamed.

"You write the boys' names on slips of paper. Each girl draws a name. Then she goes into a closet for seven minutes with the boy whose name she's drawn," Karen explained, popping a cracker into her mouth and smiling.

"What an awesome idea!" Nancy Hersh said.

"Intense!" said Karla.

"Have you noticed how people are already starting to sound like her?" Kate whispered in my ear. "I hope it isn't catching."

Chapter
6

We didn't play Truth or Dare that night, and I didn't even mention another of our sleepover games, Mad Libs. If Karen thought Truth or Dare was baby-ish, can you imagine what she would have said about Mad Libs?

Instead, we learned some of the latest dance steps from — guess where — California. Then Karen told us a really creepy story about vampires living in the sewers in L.A. I went to sleep after counting at least six girls at the party who were already saying L.A. instead of Los Angeles.

I dreamed about Jenny Carlin. She was dressed in black. She turned into a vampire and chased me to California, where Pete Stone and Karen Lawson were acting in a movie together. It was awful! I woke up with the sun shining through the window into my eyes. I had a splitting headache. I groaned to myself and massaged my throbbing temples.

"Me, too," Kate whispered. "I've been awake for hours, having Excedrin Headache Number 102: the visitor from California."

"I've had it with this sleepover," I murmured. "I don't even care about breakfast. Are you ready to go home?"

"You bet." Kate crawled out of her sleeping bag, and we crept around the bundled-up bodies of the other girls, then down the hall to the bathroom.

While we washed our faces and brushed our teeth, we talked about Karen Lawson.

"There's something funny about her," Kate said.

"Like what?" I asked.

"I'm not sure." Kate shook her head. "It's as though she's not quite real."

"It's probably just that we're not used to people from California. She must be real for California," I said.

"She's real, all right — ask Mark, or Alan, or Bobby!" said a voice. It was Stephanie, poking her head around the bathroom door. "But I know what Kate means. Maybe Karen had a personality transplant. Could this be the same girl who Patti said read

51

all the time and was very quiet? She hasn't stopped talking since she got here, except to sleep!"

"Poor Patti," Kate said. "Stuck with Karen Lawson for the whole vacation!"

"Poor Patti? Patti thinks Karen is wonderful!" said Stephanie. "Karen's going to help her loosen up!"

"Karen certainly had Pete acting like an idiot!" I slammed my toothbrush down.

"He'll get over it," Kate predicted.

"Too late," I said. "I'll never be able to forget that goofy look on his face."

"You weren't sneaking off without me, were you?" Stephanie was brushing her teeth as fast as she could. "You're not leaving me here with the California Chamber of Commerce!"

"Stephanie, have you still got that magazine we were reading at your house last Friday?" Kate asked suddenly. *Star Turns?*"

"I threw it out — why?"

"Maybe they have a copy at the library. I want to take another look at it," Kate said.

"You don't need a magazine — just ask Karen about anything," Stephanie said snippily. "She knows it, or she's seen it, or she's met it."

"Does this have something to do with your 'hmmm' last night?" I asked Kate.

"Maybe. . . ." Kate stared into space, lost in thought.

"So we'll stop at the library!" Stephanie said, dragging a comb through her curly hair. "Only let's get out of here before anybody else wakes up."

Too late — there was a knock at the door. "Can I come in?" Patti asked in her soft voice.

"Hi, Patti — we were just . . ." Stephanie began.

Patti's face fell. "You're not leaving, are you? I was hoping we could plan a tour around Riverhurst today for Karen, the way you did for me in the beginning! Charlie's and Main Street, and the mall. . . ."

"Uh — I think I . . ." I fumbled. But I didn't have the heart to say no to Patti, and neither did Stephanie or Kate. "I think I can, if everybody else can."

We had time for a quick nap at home that morning, to catch up on our sleep. Then, early in the afternoon, Mrs. Jenkins drove the five of us to Main Street, where we started hitting the hot spots of Riverhurst.

At first Karen seemed to be having a good time.

53

She liked Charlie's. "Real stained glass!" she said. "And wooden booths! There aren't many old places in Los Angeles — practically everything is brand-new. This is nice."

We ordered our usuals: float, chocolate milk shake, banana smoothie. . . .

The waitress recognized Patti. "Hey — aren't you the kid who drank a Secret Weapon last week? Lived to tell the tale, huh? Want another one?"

"It wouldn't be a new experience anymore." Patti stuck with her lime freeze, and Karen asked for a strawberry soda.

Unfortunately, Karen spilled a little of it on the sweater she was wearing. She was really upset! "Lisa's going to kill me . . ." she murmured.

"Lisa?" said Kate.

"Uh . . . yeah," Karen said, rubbing furiously at the pink spot with her napkin. "Lisa's always yelling at me for . . . for being a slob."

But the waitress brought a damp towel and scrubbed the stain out.

We picked through the sale clothes at Dandelion. Almost everything left in the pile was brown. "Just waiting for Karla to give them a good home," was how Stephanie put it.

The sidewalks were cleared of snow, but it was

cold and windy, so we caught a bus to the mall. At the Record Emporium we listened to the Boodles album at full volume on headphones until our ears rang. Then we checked out the Hawaiian shirts and surfer shorts at Just Juniors. At Pets of Distinction, we tapped on the window at three fluffy kittens.

"Is this what you do on a regular Saturday?" Karen asked then, sounding a little disappointed.

"Yes — ride our bikes, shop, hang out at the mall, go to the movies," Kate replied.

"I love movies!" Karen said.

"Want to go this afternoon?" Patti asked.

"The Riverhurst Twin Cinema is just down the street," Stephanie told Karen.

"Let's!" Karen said. "Who's calling the boys?"

"Boys?" Kate repeated.

"You don't go to the movies without boys, do you? Never mind — I'll call some. I'll start with Pete Stone. Does anybody have his number?"

Patti, Kate, and Stephanie looked at me. Then they looked anywhere else. A red flush was starting to creep up Patti's neck and out of her hair.

"I'll get it from information." Karen stopped at a phone booth and asked the operator for the number of Peter Stone, which also happened to be Pete's father's name. "Five-five-five-four-eight-nine-two?

55

Thanks." Karen dropped some change into the phone and started dialing.

I couldn't believe it. We were all just standing there watching her, while she called the boy I liked!

"Karen . . ." Patti said urgently. "Karen!" Patti tugged on Karen's sleeve, but Karen pulled her arm away. "Five-five-five-four . . ."

"That's okay, Patti," I said. "I don't have time to go to the movies this afternoon — I have to pack to visit my grandmother."

During winter vacation, my brother Roger and I usually spend four or five days with our grandmother Hunter in Bellvale. And — unless Karen Lawson's prediction about a trip not working out was right — we were leaving the next morning.

After the dopey way Pete had acted at the skating rink, Karen could have him, anyway.

"Hello, Mrs. Stone?" Karen said to Pete's mother in her breathy little voice. "Is Pete there? My name is Karen Lawson. I'm a friend of his from California."

I realized I was holding my breath.

"He is? That's great. Thank you."

Pete got to the phone in two seconds flat!

"Pete, this is Karen Lawson. Remember me?"

I guess funny old Pete must have made a joke then, because Karen laughed. "Well, I'm glad. Listen, there are five of us here, and we don't want to go to the movies by ourselves — "

"Excuse me." I spoke up loudly. "Four of us. I'm leaving."

"Oh! Do you have to?" Karen said, pouting a little.

"I'm leaving, too," said Kate.

"Then there are just three of us," Karen said into the phone, with a little wave at Kate and me. "We need you, and two more boys for Stephanie and Patti."

Karen glanced at Patti and lowered her voice, but we all heard her anyway. "Try to get Todd Farrell, okay?"

Patti's blush had faded, but it bloomed again immediately, redder than ever.

Karen was still talking.

"I'm awfully sorry, Lauren." Patti looked really upset. "Karen doesn't know that you like Pete — I should have told her."

"Don't, okay? And don't worry, Patti. I'd rather find out what kind of rotten person Pete is now than wait until later," I answered, trying to believe it myself.

"Please don't forget — the sleepover's at my house next Friday," Patti said.

Stephanie walked to the entrance with Kate and me. "The only reason I'm staying here is to keep Patti out of trouble," she said. "I'll call you later."

"Well, that's that," I said to Kate as we hopped on a bus outside the mall.

"Not quite," Kate said. "I still want to stop at the library."

The Riverhurst Public Library saves most magazines for at least three months. Not that they're organized about it, it took Kate and me a while to go through all the shelves. But I finally found the last month's copy of *Star Turns* pushed against the back wall.

"Here it is," I said to Kate. "The one with Malibu on the front."

"Horoscope . . . horoscope," Kate mumbled, flipping the pages. "Ha! 'Hortense's Horoscopes!' Listen to this. 'If you're a Pisces, you're a dreamer. You have a strong imagination. . . .' blah, blah. Okay. 'A trip you've been counting on might not work out this month, but you'll make a new friend, and smooth some ruffled feathers.' Sound like anyone you've heard recently?"

"Karen Lawson! She stole it from this magazine!"

Kate nodded. "When she was telling you your

horoscope last night, it seemed to ring a bell. And what about Joel Kelly and Carter Grant? Here's a picture of them, jogging at Malibu!" Kate's left eyebrow started its upward trip toward her hairline.

"Karen could have seen them," I argued.

"Maybe — and maybe she could have seen Kevin DeSpain and Marcy Monroe in a café on the beach." Kate held up another magazine with that very scene on the cover. "But she couldn't have met Zoltan, with the tattoos on his bald head."

"Why not?" I asked.

"Because at the end of Hortense's Horoscopes, it says that Zoltan died three hundred and fifty years ago — in Asia Minor!"

"Karen could have met another Zoltan," I said weakly.

"Come on, Lauren," Kate replied. "What does it sound like to you?"

"You mean Karen's lying?"

"At least half the time, give or take a few percent," Kate answered.

"That's really intense!" I squealed.

"Ssh!" the librarian scolded.

Chapter
7

"Karen is making it all up?" Stephanie exclaimed when she called that evening.

"Not necessarily everything. But Kate thinks she's making up at least fifty percent of what she says," I replied.

"But why? Karen's really pretty, and the boys go crazy over her," Stephanie said. "Why does she bother to lie?"

"You got me," I said. "What happened at the movies?"

"It was so awful that it was kind of funny!" Stephanie giggled. "I guess it was just an accident that Pete was home when Karen called him, because all the rest of the guys were out. Mark and Larry were sledding, Bobby and Alan had driven into the city with Mr. Krieger, Henry had to baby-sit, and Todd wouldn't come."

"I like Todd's style," I said.

"Pete couldn't find anybody."

"So what happened? Did Pete show up by himself?"

"No, he . . ." Stephanie burst out laughing. ". . . he . . . he brought Robert and Arnold Ellwanger."

Then I started to laugh, too. Robert Ellwanger is the biggest nerd in Riverhurst. One of our worst dares is daring somebody to call up Robert Ellwanger. At one of our sleepovers, Stephanie dared Kate to ask him over. Luckily, Robert said no. Not long after that, Kate dared Stephanie to ask him to the movies — and Robert said yes. Stephanie had been putting him off ever since.

"You finally had your dream date at the movies with Robert," I teased. "But who is Arnold Ellwanger?"

"Robert's first cousin from Eastport, who's staying with him this vacation." Stephanie groaned. "If Robert is the biggest nerd in Riverhurst, then Arnold is the biggest nerd in the whole state . . . in all of North America!"

"So Arnold was Patti's date, and Robert was yours." I didn't like to think about what came next, but I couldn't help it. "And Pete was Karen's."

"We-l-l-ll, it didn't really work out that way," Stephanie said.

"What do you mean?"

"It was a good movie: *Invasion from Erigeron V.* But Karen is one of those people who talks all of the way through it."

"Kate would have strangled her!" I said. Kate is very serious about films, and she hates it when anyone talks during one, even a TV movie. I mean, she doesn't like it when we talk during *commercials*!

"Well, I thought Pete was going to strangle Karen," Stephanie said. "By the end, he'd moved as far away from Karen as he could get and still be sitting with us."

I snickered. "Who was listening to Karen?"

At the same time, we shrieked, *"Robert and Arnold Ellwanger!"*

Roger and I did take a trip to our grandmother's the next day. She lives on an old farm, so we did cross-country skiing, and went ice-skating on a frozen pond, and took sleigh rides. We had a great time, but I kept wondering about what was going on back in Riverhurst with Karen Lawson and Patti and everybody else.

Dad picked Roger and me up on Thursday and drove us home. I couldn't wait to get on the phone with Kate.

"How was your trip?" she wanted to know.

"Fine," I said hurriedly. "But what's happening with Karen Lawson?"

Kate lowered her voice. "I ran into her at the mall yesterday with Patti — and they were both trying on lipstick!"

"You're kidding!" Patti in lipstick?

"Malibu Rose," Kate said darkly. "Of course. And that's not all. Patti had borrowed Karen's rubber mini, and she was wearing pink eyeshadow!"

"Are you sure Patti wasn't just blushing?"

"Only on her eyelids? Absolutely not!" Kate declared.

"Her mother would kill her!" I said. "I think Karen's a terrible influence on Patti. Something has to be done."

"And we're the ones to do it!" Kate said firmly. "At the sleepover, tomorrow night."

Kate and Stephanie and I live on Pine Street. Patti's house is on Mill Road, about four blocks away.

It was still too snowy for bikes, so, after dinner, Kate's mom drove all three of us over. It gave us a little more time to plan what we were going to say.

In fact, I'd begun to wonder if we should say anything at all. "Karen's leaving on Sunday, and that'll be the end of it," I told Kate and Stephanie. "Why should we embarrass Patti by telling her that her old friend is such a liar?"

"Because Patti thinks Karen is so wonderful and carefree and cool that she'll spend the rest of her life trying to be more like the big fake!" Stephanie said.

"Speaking of fakes, I thought you could spot a phony a mile away," Kate said to Stephanie.

Before Stephanie could answer back, I broke in. "Instead of arguing, would you mind telling me what we're going to do?"

"First we'll give Karen a chance to confess to us on her own," Kate said. "Talk about California, about astrology, about movie stars."

"And when that doesn't work?" asked Stephanie, still a little annoyed.

"Then Karen will play Truth or Dare whether she wants to or not," Kate replied.

When we pulled up out front, Patti's little brother, Horace, was building a snowman on the lawn. The snowman was tall and square, with a shiny piece of metal across its face, and nuts and bolts for eyes.

"It's a snow robot," Horace explained. "Awesome, isn't it?"

"*Awesome?* From a seven-year-old? I think we're already too late!" Stephanie hissed.

We rang the bell, and Patti opened the door. She was wearing a purple stretch jumpsuit none of us had ever seen before, and she'd pulled her hair back on both sides. It didn't even look like Patti.

"Hi guys!" she said. She looked awfully happy to see us. "Let's bring your stuff up to my room. Karen's been changing things around," she added, much less enthusiastically.

Karen certainly *had* been changing things around. Patti's room is small and cozy. The last time we'd seen it, she'd had a double bed covered with a quilt that her grandmother made and floor-to-ceiling bookshelves crammed with all kinds of neat things — books, of course, and also stuffed animals from when she was a kid, china figurines from all over the world, and very old family photographs.

Since then, the bed had been shoved into a corner. It had a new blue spread printed with yellow lines and green squiggles. The spread was okay, but it wasn't Patti. And the bookcases were almost empty! Half the books were gone, the figurines were spaced one or two to a shelf, and all of the stuffed animals had disappeared.

"What happened to Billy?" I asked Patti. Billy is a brown-and-white bear Patti got for her third birthday, and he's lived in her room ever since then.

Patti pointed up at the ceiling. "In the attic. Karen thought my room looked like it belonged to a first-grader."

"Where is Karen?" Kate inquired.

"She asked my dad to drive her to the Akura Japanese restaurant to buy some snacks for tonight," Patti answered.

"And here they are!" Karen waltzed through the door carrying four or five little white cardboard containers. "Hello, Kate, Stephanie, Lauren."

"We'll need plates, and forks, and drinks," Patti said hastily. "Lauren, will you help me?"

As we started down the stairs, Patti said in a low voice, "Lauren, can I talk to you for a second?"

"Sure. What's the problem?"

"I guess *I* am," Patti said gloomily, pulling me into the kitchen and closing the door. "I know Karen's just trying to help me, but. . . ."

There was a mournful meow from under the table. Patti kneeled down to pick up her black-and-

66

white kitten. "What is it, Tanya? Are you lonesome?"
She gave the kitten a hug.

"*Tanya?* I thought her name was *Adelaide*!" I
said.

"Karen thinks Adelaide is kind of a boring, old-
fashioned name," Patti replied. "That's the trouble — Karen is great the way she is, and I wish I
could be more like her, but I can't be, no matter how
hard I try." She looked down at the jumpsuit. "Like
these clothes! I feel dumb in them. I'm never going
to loosen up. Lauren, you're looking at an uptight
failure!"

"Stop it!" I scolded. "We all like you just the
way you are. Besides, maybe Karen's not as great as
she looks — or sounds."

"What do you mean?" Patti peered up at me.
"All of the boys think she's wonderful!"

"Not Todd Farrell," I pointed out. "She scares
him to death."

"The girls at Jane's party did."

"Sure, Karen has plenty going for her. But, Patti,
Karen's lying about a lot of things."

I told Patti about the horoscopes in *Star Turns*,
and about Zoltan, who would be about four hundred
years old now if he were alive, and about the strong

possibility that Karen saw Joel and Carter and Kevin and Marcy in magazines, not in Malibu.

"Why would Karen do that?" Patti said, puzzled. "People would like her whether she knew horoscopes, or saw movie stars, or not. It doesn't make sense."

"Kate's going to try to find out," I said. "That may be what she's up to right now!"

"We'd better get upstairs, quick!" Patti said.

She was right: When Kate wants to get to the bottom of something, she won't be sidetracked, not even by rules of common politeness. Patti pulled some forks out of a drawer, I grabbed some plates off the counter, and we raced up the stairs.

"That's right," Karen was saying as we rushed through the bedroom door. "I studied with Zoltan for several months — one or two hours a day, after school."

"Zoltan, the one with the bald head with star maps tattooed on it?" Kate asked.

"Yes." Karen was beginning to look uncomfortable.

"But, Karen," Kate said, "you couldn't have —"

She was interrupted by a lot of noise downstairs: the doorbell ringing, Patti's mom answering the door, excited voices.

"We didn't expect you so soon!"

"We finished earlier than we thought. . . ."

And more sharply, "Mrs. Jenkins, where's Karen?"

Karen stood up. "Listen, I've got to . . . uh . . ." Her eyes darted around the room, as if she were looking for a place to hide.

But footsteps pounded up the stairs. "Karen? Karen! Are you in there?"

"I think that's Karen big sister," whispered Patti. "And boy does she sound mad!"

The door to Patti's room flew open, and a teenage girl hurtled into the middle of us.

"Lisa?" Patti tried to introduce us, but Lisa Lawson didn't give her the chance.

She pointed accusingly at Karen. "You stole my clothes!"

Karen's sister was small — not much bigger than Karen — and very blonde, with spiky hair and dark eye makeup. She was wearing a black and white sweater, a black rubber mini, black tights, and long, dangly earrings. And she was angry!

"Those are *my* stretch pants!" she snapped at Karen, "and my earring." Then she glared at Patti. "And my purple jumpsuit."

"It-it is?" Patti stammered. "I didn't know . . ."

Lisa frowned crossly at the rest of us, as though

69

she expected to find us wearing her sweaters, or skirts, or something. "Obviously Karen raided my suitcase before we left California. And I didn't find out until I unpacked that first night." She scowled at Karen. "I had to wear the same clothes *two and three times!*"

"Sorry, Lisa," Karen said quietly. "I was just so tired of looking the way I usually look — boring."

"If my stuff isn't back in my suitcase in five minutes, you're . . . you're terminated!" Earrings swinging, Lisa flounced out of the room and stamped down the stairs.

Chapter
8

"Wow!" said Stephanie.

"Think it's easy, having such a cool sister?" Karen said glumly. She opened her suitcase and took out some jeans and a navy-blue sweater that was a lot like one of Patti's. "Well, I can tell you, it's not!"

Patti had grabbed a sweat shirt and sweat pants out of her closet. She couldn't get rid of the purple jumpsuit soon enough.

"I'm supposed to be the smart one in the family. I do well in school — I've always gotten great grades," Karen went on. "And Lisa's the popular one."

"Come on, Karen. You're really pretty," Kate said. "I can't believe you have any problems being popular."

"What boy is going to be interested in the smartest girl in class?" Karen folded up Lisa's pants. "I thought this trip might give me a chance to be a different person — not Karen Lawson, class brain, but Karen Lawson, the cool girl from California that everybody likes."

"Personality transplant," I murmured to Stephanie. "You were right."

"So you made up the horoscopes," Kate said.

"I read them in a magazine," Karen answered. "And the stories about Joel Kelly and Carter Grant and Kevin DeSpain? I've never seen them. I've never even seen Malibu — it's too far from where we live."

"You read it all in *Star Turns*," Stephanie guessed.

Karen nodded. "That's what got me started. There was a quiz in last month's issue about being careful or carefree."

"What was your score?" Patti wanted to know.

"I'm not telling, but the chart said I'd better check my breathing!"

"Me, too!" exclaimed Patti.

"So I thought I'd be Lisa — talk like her, dress like her, just be like her." Karen looked at me then. "I'm really sorry about Pete Stone, Lauren. I sort of figured out about you and him when we were at the movies. He talked about you a lot!"

"No big deal," I said, sounding as casual as I

could. Pete might have been a jerk at the skating rink, but there was still hope for him.

"It all kind of worked. But you know what?" Karen asked thoughtfully. "I'm glad it's over. It's exhausting being somebody else all the time."

"So — now that *that's* settled — what should we do?" Stephanie asked.

"It's *sleepover time*!" Patti shouted.

"I'm starving," I said. "What have we got to eat?"

"Lauren's always hungry," Kate told Karen.

"And she eats and eats, and never gains an ounce," Stephanie added. "It's disgusting!"

"Are you lucky," Karen said to me. "I'm so short that if I even look at food. . . ." She puffed out her cheeks.

"Me, too!" Stephanie said, eyeing the Japanese takeout cartons. "What's in the little boxes?"

"Sushi," Karen said, opening them up and lifting out small rectangles or rice wrapped in something pink or white or gray.

"I recognize the rice," Kate said. "But what's the stuff lying on top?"

"Raw fish: tuna, sea trout, mackerel, and these are salmon eggs —"

"They look like miniature bath beads," Kate said.

"And this is octopus. . . . Very non-fattening."

Octopus!

"According to that quiz in *Star Turns*, I know we're supposed to dig right in," Kate said, poking the octopus doubtfully.

"Let's order pizza!" Patti said.

"With everything?" Karen asked.

"Yep!"

"All-l-l ri-i-ight!" Karen shouted.

Patti's black and white kitten slipped around the door just then. With an excited "mew!", she trotted over to the sushi. "Adelaide," Karen said, "it's all yours."

"We'll finish the pizza," said Stephanie, "and then we'll bring all of Patti's books and animals down from the attic. . . ."

"And then we'll play Mad Libs!" Karen said. "I'm a real Mad Libs freak. I have a great idea for a really funny one!" She grabbed a notebook off Patti's desk. "I need a noun . . ."

"Quilt," said Patti.

"An adjective . . ."

"Starving," Kate said.

"A noun," said Karen.

"Kitten," I said.

"March sixteenth — you're a Quilt. You're always starving to the kitten around you . . ." Karen began.

March sixteenth is my birthday. . . .

"Lauren, it's your horoscope!" said Kate.

And we all burst out laughing.